Marble

'A resolute novel that, by virtue of its mix of literary suggestion, aesthetic experience and art historical insight, makes something that is simultaneously straightforwardly concrete and almost incomprehensibly abstract come alive.'
  – *Jyllands-Posten* ✶✶✶✶✶

'*Marble* is not reminiscent of much else, but that does not make it odd. Just beautifully its own. It is made of the stuff art and literature is made of. In excess.'
  – *Berlingske* ✶✶✶✶✶

'Amalie Smith brings marble to life.'
  – *Politiken* ❤❤❤❤❤

'Everything connects. In that Ali Smith/Isabel Waidner way, Amalie Smith manages to stuff a lot of topics in an economic way... Enriching and rewarding.'
  – *The Bobsphere*

'Admirably vivid.'
  – *Information*

'In Smith's universe, life's big and small questions are flipped and turned with exceptional artistic dexterity. Images and text often interweave into a strongly unified expression, be it when she delivers a characteristic of marble or examines the qualities of the three-dimensional. Her literary as well as visual work is distinguished by combining strong intellectual reflection on aesthetics, language and life with heart and a voice that touches and moves the viewer/reader.'
  – Jury for the Danish Crown Prince Couple's
    Rising Star Award

'*Marble* is an artistically ambitious and original attempt at creating an open, hybrid and 'impure' strand of novel which integrates and supplements fiction with factual and documentary elements... Amalie Smith digs into the material with knowledge, sensuality, and aesthetic sensibility.'
   – *Litteratursiden*

'*Marble* is a novel about insisting on the significance of surfaces, about longing and absorption, about diving and becoming porous. The book thinks across disciplines and aesthetic genre conventions, and hence it is no coincidence that Amalie Smith is a practising artist as well as a writer.'
   – *Vagant*

Lolli Editions

Translated from the Danish
by Jennifer Russell

Amalie Smith

Marble

DANIEL FOUND HER IN the ground.

He dug her free and brushed off the dirt. He joined the pieces, logged the pigment traces: how they were distributed across her clothes and her skin. Her blue-green eyes. Her coral lips. He carved new marble and filled the holes where fragments had been lost.

Her name is Marble. Daniel calls her Maggi.

'Maggi.'

Her body fills with blood that can flow in every direction.

Daniel places her on the bed. He asks what it feels like to be her. She says that her ears are small microphones. When he strokes her earlobe, it sounds like wind through a wind muffler. Now the blood flows to her legs.

Daniel lies down and Marble turns to face him. Her right hand grasps his left thigh, she pulls it across her hip. His left hand closes around her right breast.

She finds his mouth in a darkness that comes from her own closed eyes. A kiss so deep and honest, like slowly opening an abyss with your tongue. Massaging it forth.

Marble pulls back her tongue.

'Daniel, what do you see behind your closed eyes?' she asks.

'Orchids,' he says and looks more closely. 'Orchids spread throughout enormous greenhouses. And fluorescent tubes that twist through amber honey. A hand pressing small lumps of charcoal and coral into the sand on a long, white beach. And colours that seep into other colours, quickly and almost imperceptibly.'

'I see sculptures when I close my eyes,' says Marble. 'Ancient sculptures with brilliantly painted surfaces. Not just one colour, but a multitude of saturated colours covering the form. Polychrome. A surplus of colour.'

'The colour isn't superfluous,' says Daniel.

'It isn't superficial, either,' says Marble.

Now the moon casts a window of light onto the floor. Marble gets out of bed and sits on the floor and looks at the moon's window.

She lights a cigarette and blows white smoke out into the moonlight. The smoke doesn't smell of anything. She passes the cigarette to Daniel in the bed. They take turns smoking.

Marble with the cigarette pinched against the loose skin between her fingers, the entire palm of her hand beneath her chin.

'Forms are eternal,' she says. 'And materials are eternal. It's when they meet that time begins.'

Daniel blows a smoke figure that looks like a horse's head.

'You can carve a form in marble and let it travel through the centuries,' he says. 'It never stops occupying a space in the world.'

'Yes,' says Marble and blows at the horse head. 'But the colour slips off.'

Dear Laila,

If the surface is where an object ends, then nothing can be kept there. If you try to pinpoint it, it becomes thinner and thinner until it's nothing but an idea. The surface seems to border on the immaterial.

And yet we perceive the world by virtue of its surfaces. We encounter the outermost layer of things, never anything but that – through reflection, resonance, touch. Are we then only encountering ideas? Do we reach out and touch them all the time?

Daniel and I visited the cast collection today, in the warehouse down by the harbour. We wanted to take a closer look at the cast surfaces. To reproduce a form in plaster, you solidify the air around it. Then you cast the copy inside the cavity. That is to say, you turn the form around its own immaterial surface.

The collection consists of three stories crammed with plaster copies of European sculpture. We wandered around among the copies as if they were something other than plaster in familiar forms. *The Laocoön Group, Venus de Milo* etc. The form transcended the plaster like an echo that said: You've seen me before. I was deeply moved. I couldn't help but touch the plaster. I thought: The plaster does not know what it represents, and yet it has the potential to represent anything.

But then Daniel pointed out something black within the folds of the sculptures, and said: That's time.

And: The muzzle of the Parthenon horse head shines because the plaster has drunk from the hands that have touched it.

The casts' surfaces have a history. They were kept at the Academy of Fine Arts, where they gathered dust and were painted white instead of being cleaned, and later exhibited at the National Gallery. Again and again they were deemed worthy of being touched and reproduced and restored.

I said: But these sculptures were created white. There are no traces of paint.

Then we noticed the painted plaster of the Greek korai statues. And Anne Marie Carl-Nielsen's coloured reproductions from the Acropolis: the Typhon and the Bull's Head.

So everything wasn't white after all.

Anne Marie Carl-Nielsen!

Say hello from me in New York,

MARBLE

'A DIGITAL 3D MODEL consists purely of surfaces. Nothing solid exists in three-dimensional space. Nothing fluid or ethereal. It isn't possible to model a landscape without surfaces,' says the 3D animator.

But that's exactly what Marble wants: a landscape without surfaces.

'The empty space has no surfaces,' the 3D animator adds and points at the screen.

The screen shows a dark-grey plane. Three coloured axes, one green, one blue and one red, diverge from a point at the centre of the screen. The axes indicate width, height and depth.

The 3D animator can reach into the screen's three-dimensional picture plane with her mouse and keyboard. She can twist and turn a given 3D model on the screen. Enlarge and shrink it. Cut and drag it. Animate it and make it speak.

'The empty space is too much,' says Marble. 'Too many points where the emptiness refers to itself.'

'OK,' says the 3D animator and creates a sphere that looks like a ping-pong ball. She shrinks it drastically and replicates it millions of times. Using a randomised algorithm, she distributes the spheres throughout the space. Together they form something that resembles vapour.

The vapour is white, the background is charcoal grey.

'Thank you,' says Marble. 'I will now journey through that vapour.'

'Safe journey,' says the 3D animator.

Marble travels through this landscape of vapour and discovers that it is a landscape without surfaces.

The vapour is neither wet nor dry; it has neither sound nor smell. It condenses and expands with the unpredictability of a landscape.

Then a face emerges from the vapour. A woman's face with thin lips and friendly, bright eyes. A primitive animation.

She floats in front of Marble without a word.

IN THE SPRING OF 1903 Danish sculptor Anne Marie Carl-Nielsen travels to Athens on a grant, and her husband, the composer Carl Nielsen, accompanies her.

She goes to Athens because she wants to copy Archaic sculptures discovered during the excavation of the Acropolis in the 1880s.

Italian cast-maker Napoleone Martinelli has a monopoly on the production of casts of ancient sculpture in Greece. But the sculptures found at the Acropolis have such well-preserved colours that they cannot be used as moulds, as the process would remove the paint.

Marie is granted permission to make copies of the sculptures in clay, create moulds on the basis of the clay sculptures, and then cast plaster reproductions in the moulds.

There's a photograph of her and Carl taken at the old Acropolis Museum. The photograph documents her copy of the Typhon: an Archaic pediment sculpture of a monster with three truncated torsos and three bearded male heads. The first two heads from the left look towards the middle of the pediment, where two lions are bringing down a bull, while the third looks out at the viewer. The monster's lower body consists of intertwined snake tails that twist towards the pediment's right corner.

A magnificent piece of primitive open-air sculpture with bold forms and childlike strength and variegated colour all the way to the outermost twist of its tail! writes Danish archaeologist Frederik Poulsen of the Typhon in 1929, in the book *Early Greek Art*.

The photograph has no colour, but it has nine faces: three originals in limestone, four in plaster, and then Marie and Carl's faces, which are dark grey, that is, suntanned. Marie is wearing a white, full-length linen dress; Carl is in a black suit with white cuffs.

What's Carl doing in the picture? His face is turned in a different direction than the other eight faces. He's sitting on a stool in front of Marie, right beneath the copy of the Typhon. He has taken off his straw hat and is holding it in his hand.

She began working on the copy in March, and it has now taken form; perhaps we're in June 1903. It's hot at the museum.

Marie holds an extra copy of the monster's third head in her hands, and it looks as though its stiff beard is resting on top of Carl's head.

Some water has leaked from a vase out onto the marble floor.

One might think she were nearly done, but she's not. She'll have to return in November the following year and work for seven more months. That's when Carl writes her a letter saying he wants a divorce.

But before that, she sends the photograph to museums across Europe, asking whether anyone would like to commission casts. They would. The still nascent body of European museums is eager to acquire reproductions of all these classical sculptures. That way people will be able to come and see them in plaster, at the new National Gallery of Denmark, for example. They'll be able to walk all the way around them and grasp the ancient origins of their own culture, without the arousing translucency and polished sheen of marble, so evocative of skin. Plaster is dry and dead and more modest than marble.

Marie paints her plaster reproductions. But in spring of 1903 she is yet to begin painting. She and Carl have taken up residence at Hotel Achilleion, where they live off her grant. When the Acropolis Museum opens, Marie goes up there to work. She stands in the middle of the exhibition. The lighting is poor. Each day she transfers more of the Typhon's form to the clay, recreating its porous surfaces and fractures.

Great precision is required to reproduce a fracture. It requires a different logic than when modelling carved surfaces.

DANIEL AND MARBLE BORROW a car and drive south to the limestone quarry outside the town of Faxe. At the quarry is a small museum where they see a black-and-white photograph of a house dusted white by the smoke from the lime kiln; white roof, white grass, white laundry on the clothesline.

They stand at the vantage point behind the museum and look out across the quarry. The sun is shining and the white surface reflects all the colours. The quarry lakes mirror an ice-blue sky.

It's Sunday, and the excavators and conveyor belts that on weekdays extract the limestone, process it and sort it into piles according to particle size, now stand still.

Daniel and Marble descend into the quarry by foot. It's quiet down there. They can hear the croaking of hundreds of frogs next to a whitewashed and ice-blue shore. And someone splitting the limestone. Ding – ding – ding.

A middle-aged couple in sandals and caps comes into view from behind a big pile of limestone; they carry tools and buckets. Marble and Daniel can hear fragments of the couple's conversation even though they're far away and speaking softly. They're speaking in German to each other. Sound travels easily in a mineral landscape.

The couple sits down and carries on splitting the limestone.

Daniel walks over to them. Marble sits down by a lake and listens to the frogs' mating calls. We've dug into another era, she thinks. She hears Daniel talking to the couple.

He returns with something wrapped in a German leaflet. Marble unwraps it. It's a lump of limestone that has been split.

'Limestone?'

'Yes. Look carefully.'

She holds it up and peers into a criss-cross of tiny fossilised white skeletons, branch-shaped, sausage-shaped, tube-shaped. Structures so delicate it's hard to believe they weren't crushed long ago.

'Faxe coral,' says Daniel. 'There was a coral reef here 63 million years ago.'

'Here?'

'Yes, and it's still here. We're walking among the ossified skeletons of the coral reef.'

'Skeletons?' asks Marble. 'Is coral an animal?'

'A coral reef consists of polyps that create a shared skeleton across generations,' says Daniel. 'The Germans told me. They're amateur geologists.'

Marble turns the lump of limestone over and tiny fossil fragments sprinkle out.

'If corals share a common skeleton produced across generations, could the entire coral reef not be considered a single organism?' wonders Marble.

'Why do you ask?'

'Because that would mean we're standing in the middle of one gigantic skeleton,' she says.

Daniel laughs.

A chill runs down Marble's spine. She doesn't know whether it's the many small skeletons or the single enormous one that makes her uneasy.

Just then a fighter jet flies over the quarry. At first it appears as an image, so close they can see its underside: the joints of the metal plates. A brief glimpse of a different scale – very big, very close, very fast. Then comes the sound: a long blast that lingers in the quarry long after the image of the jet has disappeared.

'WILL YOU HELP ME recreate a form with 3D software?' asks Marble.

'Sure,' the 3D animator replies. 'Which one?'

Marble opens a book and points at a photograph of a clay frieze.

'Anne Marie Carl-Nielsen modelled this for the pediment of King Christian IX's equestrian statue,' she says. 'It represents the Danish people under the king's rule. At the very front stand the farmer and the fisher, and behind them are representatives of trade, seafaring, industry, science and art. There are also two writers, J.P. Jacobsen with his nose in a book, and behind him, Holger Drachmann, in a cape, looking up as though it has just started to rain.'

'They're quite close together. Do you want all of them modelled?' asks the 3D animator.

'No, only the diver,' Marble says and points.

Kneeling down in the middle of the frieze is a diver, shown in profile. He wears a diving suit with a big, round helmet and thick-soled boots. He has a knife stuck in his belt and is coiling a rope with strong, fisted hands.

'Ah, I can see why. He's impressive.'

'Yes, I was looking for information about her coloured reproductions of Archaic sculptures and I stumbled across him,' Marble says. 'I'd like a negative impression of him – a mould, that is, and then I want to cast him.'

'One thing at a time. Do you have any pictures of the frieze from other angles?'

'No, this is all I have,' says Marble and points at the book.

'Then I'll have to model him from scratch using 3D software. It'll take time.'

'Just let me know when you're done.'

DANIEL WAKES UP AT night and watches Marble sleeping. Her face is relaxed. Only her eyes move beneath her eyelids.

A truly relaxed face is the face of the dead, Daniel thinks. In sleep, too, your face is on display, tautly stretched like a kite in the wind of a dream.

Marble dreams of a diver kneeling on the ocean floor. He wears a shining copper helmet and a thick canvas suit. His air hose winds underneath his arm.

The helmet is attached to the suit with bolts that Marble unscrews. She lifts off the helmet. The diver's face is shapeless like a lump of dough. It has no form.

Marble wakes up and looks at Daniel. He turns on the light. She smiles at him. He smiles back.

What do you do with reciprocated love?

'I'm going,' she says.

'Going where?' he asks.

'To Athens,' she says. 'I want to take a closer look at the surfaces of ancient sculpture.'

EVERY MATERIAL HAS A colour. The colours of some materials lie within the infrared spectrum. Infrared photography is used in polychromy research to locate traces of the pigment Egyptian blue, which fluoresces in the infrared spectrum when exposed to visible light.

Marble opens her DSLR camera, loosens the screws, jiggles off the back, dismantles the wires, breaks the solder and pushes aside a plate to get to the light-sensitive sensor. In front of the sensor is an iridescent filter that shimmers pink and cyan and blocks the infrared light. She removes it. Now the camera is sensitive to near-infrared wavelengths, 730-900 nanometres.

But the photographs she takes come out faded and yellowish. She needs a filter that blocks all visible light so only infrared light passes through.

The filter is called LEE 87. It's an opaque black filter and it's sold at B&H Photo on 9th Avenue in New York. She gets Laila to send it.

On the box it says: *Visually opaque, transmission begins above 730 nm.*

Marble adjusts the camera's aperture and exposure time, then holds the LEE filter in front of the lens and takes a picture. Through the viewfinder she sees only

darkness. On the camera's LCD screen she sees a translation. The translation is magenta-toned in a spectrum
ranging from dark magenta to white. The camera lifts
infrared light into the visible spectrum.

Dear Laila,

Art historian Alois Riegl writes that if art sought to imitate reality, it would be a simple matter: the artist would cast the given object in plaster and subsequently paint the cast.

Isn't that a lovely thought?

Instead of photography, you could perform tableaux vivants. And instead of films: total theatre. Imitative art would end where it began – with the ephemeral.

Classical art from the Renaissance and onwards did not wish to be ephemeral. Rather than attempting to imitate reality, it sought to get at the ideas behind it. Like the sciences, art began to define itself through separate disciplines. Painting became that which is without form and sculpture became that which is without colour.

Form and colour were separated. White sculpture was invented.

I think of the separation of form and colour as a compression tool intended to make possible the transportation of materials into the immortal, into the world of ideas, into eternity.

I'm afraid that ancient sculpture has been subjected to the same compression that the art of the Renaissance underwent, and, later, the Neoclassical period. After all, the sculptures have travelled through all these centuries.

I read about an Archaic (pre-classical) sculpture in Athens that is believed to have carried a scent! Phrasikleia is her name; in her hand is a lotus made of stone, and people may have dripped essential oils onto the flower.

When a group gathered in front of Phrasikleia, one of them would read aloud the pedestal inscription, and because it was written in the first person, she was given voice.

MARBLE

A DENSE FOG HAS descended over Copenhagen the morning Marble leaves. She sits in the aeroplane and watches the terminal disappear into the white. The lights of the runway shine as though the fog were darkness.

But up above, the sky is clear. Two factory chimneys jut up through the fog. The blades of three wind turbines appear and disappear like the arms of swimmers.

Europe is covered by dense white clouds. Marble alternately reads and sleeps. The pilot mentions which countries they fly 'through'.

The thing about flying is that you're disconnected from all the lives you fly over. The thought of them makes her dizzy. What kinds of radiation reach the plane? Radio waves. Satellite signals. Cosmic rays.

She reads the newspaper with a sense of *text*. Papal plane. Papal letdown. Papal pacemaker. Standard &

Poor's, Moody's and Fitch. North Korea detonated one, maybe two atomic bombs last night, deep underground.

Air France has the most beautiful cabin crew Marble has ever seen. The steward is young with flecks of grey in his hair, dressed in a well-fitting suit and a narrow red tie. His *bonjour* is like a kiss he blows, making her blush. The stewardess has her hair done up in a bun and her skin is as smooth as the airport's big billboard faces on a background of water. Her clothes are tailored: a black dress with a red sash around the waist, red leather gloves. She tidies up the cabin carrying what looks like a shopping bag.

Marble remembers how the LEE filter glided across the X-ray scanner's screen at airport security, a huge black pixel. 15 square inches of opacity.

In the infrared photograph she takes of herself in the mirror in the aeroplane lavatory, her skin looks like wax, or dull crystal. Her lips blend in with the rest of her face, her freckles are erased. Infrared light penetrates deeper into skin before being reflected than white light does.

Her hair is icy blonde and so are her eyebrows and eyelashes. Her pupils have swelled up and swallowed the irises.

The green chlorophyll in plants whitens in infrared pictures. It's called the Wood Effect. Entire landscapes whiten, like frost on grass. Sky and water darken, a nearly black magenta. In the photograph she takes from the aeroplane window, the sky looks like a night sky. A dark river meanders through the pale landscape beneath the plane.

It doesn't look like Earth but an imaginary planet, also inhabited. The fact that it *is* Earth makes her tingle inside. That you could open a door to a parallel landscape. That you could dip below the visible spectrum.

Marble falls asleep and wakes up and reads some more. When the plane banks during their approach, the sun slices through the window, illuminating her book from behind so the holes in the seam of its spine glow.

Then they descend. Beneath the clouds it's raining; the runway is wet. Gentle ribbons of rain stream down the window of the train into town. Along the tracks are big, unrented billboards that display the oxidation process of common metals.

Here is Athens, glazed with rain, its streets dissolved into fluid expanses of marble and minerals. A carved city. Everything sighs and glistens.

THE ORANGE TREES BLOSSOM into white. They don't smell of fruit but something else, a welcoming perfume. Bergamot, perhaps. Athens is warm like freshly toasted spice bread.

Marble sits on the balcony and looks at the street. The souvenir shops open and roll postcard stands out onto the pavement. They hang bunches of bath sponges beside their doors.

A young man smokes his first cigarette of the day on the balcony across from Marble's.

This isn't her city or her balcony. She lives in a home she

has borrowed. She doesn't receive mail. She doesn't pay taxes. No plumber or neighbour walks through the door.

She's alone. She *wants* to be alone.

The Greek alphabet is indecipherable but entices her with its meaning all the same. She stares at the letters on the milk carton like someone who hasn't learned to read. She *hasn't* learned to read; she guesses the names of the metro stations.

She doesn't want to learn how to read. She wants to learn how to *see*.

She sees her face in the mirror and does not recognise it right away. She touches the marble-white scars on her cheeks and below her eye: small fractures in the form that is her.

Perhaps the unbroken form exists as an idea behind the present form of her face.

'I am strong here,' she says, massaging a scar. A scar makes the skin stronger.

Her reflection blinks.

Is it possible to be happy *because* you are broken?

A SOLAR STORM SWEEPS across the city, it thunders but it doesn't rain. Marble climbs up Filopappou Hill to watch the sunset; its hues spill over into purple. The entire electromagnetic spectrum is in play. She takes an infrared photograph of the Acropolis, and in it the citadel is wreathed with cotton-white tree crowns.

Marble smokes a cigarette at the top of the hill. The ember glimmers.

She rests her head in the grass and pulls her legs to her chest. In the sunset the red poppies look redder than any poppies she's ever seen before. The flowers in the tall grass have fluorescent patterns intended for the kaleidoscope-eyes of insects.

The red beyond the mountains. The purple within the mountains. Something soft and white across the sea. The container ships sit on the water's surface as if it were sand or gravel.

Can you imagine an object so heavy it continues to sink when placed on sand?

There must be a liquid that can be poured into another liquid without the volume increasing, Marble thinks.

A liquid with enough room within it.

The hill is warm after a day of sun, it radiates heat that mixes with cooler air from higher elevations; gentle currents that intertwine in increasingly complex ways. It is at and around the air currents' surfaces that turbulence occurs.

The air isn't empty; it carries things. Tiny bits of plant material and dust that glitter in the sun.

Radiation, yes. From space, from Earth. Radio waves, telephone signals, the internet.

Daniel whispers to her from Copenhagen. She tunes her ear to the frequency of his voice.

'Maggi?'

No, she wants to be alone.

The tall grass grows opaque as dusk falls. It sways, then stands still. Dogs with long tails scamper in and out among the murky bushes. Their owners dance with ribbons. Pale strips of silk softly swishing and drums playing; not steady but tentative, listening beats.

Marble sits up and gazes out at the Acropolis. The floodlights have now been turned on. The scaffolding around the Parthenon's west side blends in with the dark blue sky. From here she cannot see the construction trailers, the cranes, the workshops and the sheds where workers eat their lunch among the ruins, but she knows they're there. That they're restoring the Parthenon, filling its holes with new marble.

The restoration carried out in the early 1900s was catastrophic. The columns were incorrectly assembled and iron was used in the joints; in Ancient Greece, they used lead. The iron rusted and expanded, the columns cracked.

When the current restoration began in 1975, it was necessary to take apart much of the temple in order to map the damage and catalogue the fragments. Later a digital archive was created, which included 3D scans of over 5,000 blocks and fragments. A three-dimensional puzzle.

How many computer programs can be used in the span of 20 years, Marble wonders. How many times have they had to switch systems, running the risk of data going lost?

'Maggi?'

The restoration follows the Venice Charter from 1964: the original marble is not modified. Marble is only added where the building's parts cannot hold and it's sourced from the Pentelicon quarry north of the city, the same quarry from which the ancient marble came. Titanium joints are used, but as sparingly as possible. Everything is reversible.

Any notion of stylistic purity, however, must be relinquished. The Venice Charter states: *The valid contributions of all periods to the building of a monument must be respected, because unity of style is not the aim of a restoration.*

'Maggi?'

The Ottomans built a mosque in the middle of the Parthenon that was later torn down. Smaller temples were erected and torn down around it, built of parts from other temples. Taken apart, taken away, brought back together. Which time do you revert to when you restore?

'Maggi, are you there?'

'Hi, Daniel.'

'There you are.'

'Yes. I've seen marble polished so it looks just like oily cheeks. Very lifelike.'

'What about the colour? Have you found traces of colour?'

'Not yet. But today I saw a woman blowing bubbles on the promenade in front of the Acropolis. She blew them in several layers so each bubble could spin around inside the next, and then she filled them with coloured smoke.'

'Ah. Didn't the smoke weigh down the bubbles?'

'It did. And when the bubbles landed on the ground, the smoke escaped and drifted away as a multicoloured cloud. You should have seen it.'

'I wish I had.'

It's getting dark and Marble has to make her way back down. The moon is thin as a nail clipping but the city illuminates the path.

A dog barks in the darkness. Marble turns towards the sound and sees figures on the ground among the bushes. People in sleeping bags. A breeze sweeps smells from the homeless people's camp onto the path – sweat that has

dried in the sun, a yeasty odour from the dogs' throats.
She's not alone. Chamomile grows along the path.

AT NIGHT ENORMOUS SHADOWS appear on the rock face of the Acropolis: outlines of plants that have crept in front of the floodlights illuminating the hill. The shadows sway in the wind, ten metres back, ten metres forth.

Marble walks south around the Acropolis. Along the fence live hundreds of cats. She has seen a woman dressed in white scatter kibble at the foot of the fence. The cats lie down and eat with their paws tucked beneath their bodies, like living porcelain figurines.

Marble has heard the cats crying at night the way babies do. Not with hunger though, but with desire.

The cats' fur is static.

Marble walks over to the fence, squats down and squints. A black cat with green eyes ambles over.

She reaches out her hand to touch its fur, catches hold of its tail and doesn't let go. The cat freezes and looks right through her the way that cats do.

'The sculptor believes you master a form by fixing it,' says the cat.

Marble loosens her grip. When the cat disappears through the fence, its tail strikes a spark.

ANNE MARIE CARL-NIELSEN GROWS up on a farm in the moraine country of Kolding with her parents, two brothers, a sister and their farm animals. Her father rears cattle and imports English sheep, which provide more wool than Danish sheep. Every spring he drives the cattle across Jutland, down to the marshes of Tønder.

She is born in 1863, on the longest day of the year, and a Sunday, at that. The world she is born into is bright and warm. She is christened Anne Marie Brodersen and called Marie. She takes in a porcupine and a baby hare as pets. A toad with glassy yellow eyes, wide as a worker's fist. When she goes riding, a crow perches on her shoulder.

She rides horses from the age of five. She experiments with standing on two horses, one foot on either horseback, until her mother asks her to stop. She's her father's favourite, always outside with the animals, kind, courageous, clever.

When she's ten, her father has the barn torn down to build a new one and her oldest brother Hans is crushed beneath a collapsing wall. A sculptural memory: she sees her father walk across the courtyard carrying her dead brother in his arms.

As a 12-year-old she digs glacial clay from the vegetable patch and models a lamb that she has hand-reared. The model is a good likeness. She continues modelling heads and animals and asks to go to school, is told no, then granted permission after all, spends three months at a woodcarving school in Schleswig, but after that it's time for her to come home. She receives a slap from her father and is told to know her place, be domestic, churn butter. But in the butter, Marie models crows.

Marie enters the world hands first. Grasping life with both hands, you could say. Sculpture is what you can approach from all sides, see from every angle.

Her father's calves get sick, Marie takes care of them. There are 42 in all, they require milk three times a day, she herds them around the farm. They recover. The veterinarian teaches her about the animals' anatomy. He gives her horse bones to model after. She dissects a dead calf and preserves it in limewater to study the composition of its muscles.

In the stable, modelled animals stand side by side with living animals, a head next to the head. She has nearly completed a clay model of a cow with a suckling calf when a wagon runs into the cow and breaks it.

She models the living, too. She obtains wax and hangs a board from her neck so she can walk around in the fields and model animals in motion. When a calf refuses to get into position, she hops over the fence to the neighbour's cows and collects lice, which she then sets loose on the family's calf to make it move.

A Calf Licking Itself, 1887. *A Calf Scratching Itself Behind Its Ear*, 1887.

What are we to do with these little bronze animals, so similar to porcelain figurines? Do they move us? Yes. Can they teach us something about the animals' lives? Yes. How they scratch themselves, how they shudder in the wind.

It's healthy animals she shows us. It's the farmer's pride in his livestock. The animals must be treated well. Humans look after them and slaughter them humanely. With the mix of haphazardness and dedication that animal husbandry involves. The animals belong to us. And yet they are not ours.

She returns to the works of her youth many years later. After marriage and children, equestrian statues and memorials, she sits down and models little animal studies out of wax from memory.

With her finger she draws a circle on the table and says:

'Here is where I started, and here is where I finished.'

'SOMETHING'S ODD ABOUT THAT diver,' says the 3D animator and points at the photograph of the frieze.

'What do you mean?' asks Marble.

'The frieze's figures are huddled together, like passengers in a streetcar or marchers in a protest. But a diver's suit like that is heavy. You can't wear it on land.'

'The diver is underwater?'

'Yes. Anne Marie Carl-Nielsen must have fused several spaces into one.'

'Maybe none of the figures occupy the same space. Maybe each person carries their own space with them?'

'Maybe,' says the 3D animator.

'But all the other figures are on land.'

'You're right,' says Marble. 'The diver is the exception. If he can dive there, he can dive anywhere.'

Behind the kneeling diver's boot is a creased trouser leg. It belongs to a man whose face is unfinished. He's turned away from the diver, looking back at Holger Drachmann.

'The frieze is a study,' says Marble. 'The judging committee asked Anne Marie Carl-Nielsen to start by modelling one side of the frieze at half size, because she had never under- taken a project of this scale before, and because she was the first woman ever commissioned to make an equestrian statue. The committee ultimately decided against the frieze, so it was never enlarged and cast in bronze.'

'But the equestrian statue was cast?'

'Yes! It was four and a half metres tall.'

Marble flips through the pages and finds a photo of Marie posing beneath the horse.

'She decided not to have it chemically patinated, as was the custom at the time. The monument was driven through the streets of Copenhagen, its bronze bright and shiny, and erected at Christiansborg Palace's riding grounds in 1927. It's still there today, patinated by rain and black on its belly.'

Dear Laila,

Here I am, in Athens. I'm sitting on the terrace of the new Acropolis Museum with a view of the Acropolis's southern slope. Along the hill's steep eastern side runs a rope hoist. A big white package on a pallet is suspended in the air.

The museum is wonderful. The building was inaugurated in 2009; it floats above an excavation site, resting on columns as wide as the Parthenon's. You walk up a big ramp in the middle of the building and arrive in the Archaic Gallery. Inside, fragmented sculptures stand on plinths of varying heights in front of enormous frosted windows. When I walk through that room, I feel as though I'm being lifted.

You continue up the escalators to the top floor where the Parthenon Frieze is exhibited, but it's only a copy. The original is at the British Museum. The rest of the Parthenon sculptures are scattered between London, Paris, Vienna, Würzburg, Munich, the Vatican and Copenhagen. The gallery is full of plaster replicas. The pediment sculptures look like frosting on a cake.

The Parthenon Frieze is from the Classical period, and its figures are flawlessly executed, but to me they look identical, like cookie cutters – one face, one body, one horse, it's rather boring.

The sculptures in the Archaic Gallery are much livelier. I'm particularly fond of the korai: statues of young women who stand with one foot in front of the other, Egyptian in their rigidity, one hand pulling at the fabric of their dress. With the other hand they extend a gift, they smile, that's all they do.

Have you seen them? I think you'd like them. They're all very different, and they aren't perfect. They vary in size and proportion, their bodies are crooked. But they aren't portraits

– rather, their bodies and faces were intended to display the sculptures' adornment. They're draped in patterned marble fabric, their hair is plaited, they wear jewellery and have inlaid eyes. And all over them there are traces of colour!

I spoke to a guide in the Archaic Gallery, his name is Vassilis. He told me that the Archaic sculptures were buried when the Persians conquered Athens, shortly after they had been painted. Earth preserves. That's why much of the paint was intact when the sculptures were dug up more than 2,000 years later.

But they've since lost their colour. Researchers can tell from watercolours painted just after the excavations. But the watercolours, they fade too.

We say that things have colours, and that their colours can fade over time. But in fact, an object absorbs all colours except for the one it reflects back at us. Colour is what leaves us. Just like the surface, colour seems to border on the immaterial.

How do you bind something as weightless as colour to the world? Pigments, sure. But pigments are ephemeral. Pulverised rock, soil and plant extracts mixed with wax or egg. They wash away with the rain. They're bleached by sun. The oxygen in the air grates at them.

Form is more durable than colour. Some sculptures were painted over several times. The colour must be retold in order to go on existing. Or it must be buried in the ground and preserved there.

Laila, it seems to me that it isn't just the paint but everything that slips away. The museum is transitory, the sculptures are transported through various buildings and exhibitions and installations. Where will the korai be in a hundred years? In a thousand?

Now I long for Daniel.

Thank you for the LEE filter, by the way. It works. I'll send pictures as soon as I've transferred them.

Tell me, is spring mild and translucent where you are? Have the trees opened their buds?

MARBLE

IN THE SUN, STEAM rises from the cobbled promenade in front of the Acropolis, like a dream slipping
from memory. The sky is covered in wispy clouds.

Marble smokes a cigarette by the entrance and watches
a team of workers pruning the promenade's trees. She
takes an infrared photo of them. The leaves on the
ground look like drifts of snow around the tree trunks.

Marble passes through the metal detector at the
entrance and slips in among the flocks of students and
tourists following their respective guides up the big
ramp in the museum's centre.

The groups stop next to the statue of Papposilenos with
Dionysus on his shoulders; he holds a marble mask in
his right hand, but his own head is missing.

You have to get used to the fragments, to the headless, armless, legless, noseless, fingerless. A famous Archaic dog recently recovered a bit more of its stumpy tail. Archaeologists knew of the tail-stump, they knew of the dog, the two pieces had never been put together.

That's what they have to work with. Bits and pieces. The guide is in white trainers and sunglasses with lenses that gleam like petrol on water. Cords to keep everything in place. He points with a laser pen.

At the end of the ramp, right as you enter the gallery, are the fragments of the Hekatompedon Temple's pediment, which stood at the Acropolis before the Parthenon. At the centre of the pediment is a bull being slain by two lions, and to the far right is the monster Typhon. The groups stop here, too. The pediment is executed in *poros*, a porous type of limestone, and heavily painted.

The groups turn right and enter the Archaic Gallery. Straight ahead is the Calf Bearer with no visible traces of paint. The Persian Rider in chequered harlequin leggings stands in front of the frosted windows. The Archaic korai are dispersed throughout the room; youthful, stiff, elegantly dressed women, holding out their votive offerings and smiling.

Marble stands in front of the Peplos Kore, who's dressed in a smooth, patterned dress. On one side of the kore stands a painted full-size replica, and on the other is a vertical LCD screen showing a digital reconstruction that revolves on its own axis. Marble turns to a man standing next to her, it's Vassilis, he's holding an iPad in his hand.

'The reconstructions are different,' notes Marble. 'On one the dress is yellow, on the other it's white.'

'Reconstructions are always interpretations,' says Vassilis. 'We can't know whether the pigment traces we find were mixed with other pigments, or whether the painter added layers to create highlights and shadows.'

'So reconstructions are fictions, too?' asks Marble.

'Partly. But they're not pure guesswork. We have various techniques to detect pigment traces that aren't visible to the eye. We use a microscope. We take X-rays. And we use raking light photography to reveal the texture of the stone's surface. And ultraviolet and infrared photographs.'

Vassilis scrolls through his iPad and shows Marble an infrared photograph of a kore. Egyptian blue gleams like shards of mirror in the marble.

'In my time here at the museum I've seen eyelashes fade and disappear,' he says. 'It's only a question of time before they won't be detectable anymore either. Perhaps it will take a couple hundred years, perhaps a couple thousand, but eventually the colours will vanish.'

'Is there anything you can do to stop it?'

'No. But we can record the traces that haven't yet disappeared.'

'But can you conserve them?'

'Repaint them? No. We make copies and reconstructions instead.'

'But what if you kept them in the dark, could you then preserve the colours?'

'Maybe, but then you wouldn't be able to see that the korai were carved in marble from Paros, which is transparent the same way skin is. It requires light to see it. The korai were meant to stand in the sun.'

Vassilis points up at the Acropolis.

Marble leans in closer to the Peplos Kore and sees how the light sinks into her arm. Her skin looks alive.

'Their skin was painted, too,' says Vassilis, pointing at the painted copy. Her arms, face and neck are painted a bright yellow-pink.

Marble looks up.

'But marble from Paros was the finest,' she said. 'The most skinlike. Why cover it up?'

'No skin is white as marble,' says Vassilis. 'Marble from Paros is the best for carving and the best for painting. Light emanates through the paint and brings it to life.'

Here Vassilis and Marble part ways. He's got a tour to give, she continues on her own.

FOR ARCHAIC KORAI, THE body and face are made to display their adornment:

The painted patterns of the garments. Broad bands of spirals and meanders. Rosettes, palmettes, volutes, crosses. A line becomes a pattern by virtue of the flowing drapery.

The stylised draping of the marble fabric. A spatial pattern that interweaves with the garments' painted patterns. The ends of the draped folds look like organ pipes; they've been hollowed out, you can bend over and peer into them. Light penetrates the thinnest folds.

The jewellery. Disc-shaped earrings, headbands. A carved and painted serpentine bracelet. Holes and marks left from tiaras and bracelets made of precious metals.

The sandals. One carved sandal and one painted. Both with thick soles. A hole for a bronze ornament on the strap across the ankle. All the things the ankle must carry. A dress clings to the calves, drapes across the foot. An elastic material, incised.

The eyes. Either painted or inlaid. Green traces of the lead used to affix eyes made of crystal or glass. The eyes' inherent depth. Painted eyelashes. Or attached, made of tin or bronze.

The hair. Crimped, carved, painted hair. It's not plaited, but rather like a chunky woven carpet that covers the neck, thickening it. Patterns that resemble the sandy seabed woven by waves.

The gifts. In outstretched, white-knuckled hands. A pomegranate. An apple. A bird.

HOW CAN A STONE become human? Stand there like a

human. Stone doesn't turn into flesh simply by being carved into the shape of a human. There's no chest beneath the dress. There's no slender neck beneath the thick hair, no soft marble throat.

But as soon as the stone is given human form, it's no longer just a stone. Suddenly it can lack a 'head' or an 'arm'. It's a human body that can be maimed.

The korai's curved, painted lips form an Archaic smile. A subtle, aloof smile. Either indulgent or knowing.

The Archaic smile is the stone's smile, thinks Marble.

She holds up the LEE filter in front of her camera's lens and takes a picture of a kore. The LCD screen shows nothing but a uniform shade of magenta. Marble opens the lens's shutter step by step. From the darkness the kore emerges. First the surfaces facing the light become visible, then she can also see the plinth and the floor. The tourists' waxen skin.

Marble walks around to the back of the kore and takes another picture. Then she sees them: traces of Egyptian blue that flare in the infrared spectrum. Tiny shards of mirror in the patterned hem of the dress.

Like when you look out across the city from the top of the Acropolis and windows here and there stand open at angles that reflect the sunlight back into your eyes.

Oh!

Her body knows it's being spoken to before her head does. Only then does she hear someone shout:

'No photos please!'

Marble has her shoulders up around her ears, camera to her eye, filter in front of the lens. Now blood rushes to her cheeks. She packs the camera away and sits down on a bench in the opposite end of the gallery.

She realises that the call is recurrent, but each time it cuts through the room from a new angle. A rough incision that's smoothed over by the strolling of tourists back and forth.

WHY IS A PERSON so absorbed and so receptive when taking a picture? Faithful and paranoid at the same time. You look through the viewfinder or at the screen and can control the frame, and yet the camera's restriction of your vision makes you vulnerable.

The camera separates and connects. It grants sight a capacity for memory that can be shared. It serves as a remote sense for people far away with less and less delay.

Marble has never seen so many people take so many pictures as the tourists at the Acropolis do. She curls up in a shell hole in the fortification wall surrounding the citadel to read and ends up in a number of that day's photographs.

Later, Daniel will be able to do an image search for the Acropolis and find her. She's ten pixels here, 20 pixels there. A speck of light on a surface. All those pictures will make him nauseous. Who will see them?

He will realise that the internet isn't weightless.

He has sent her a link to an article about an organisation called CyArk. They make detailed 3D scans of cultural world heritage sites and store them on magnetic tapes underneath what used to be a limestone mine in Pennsylvania. Should the buildings be destroyed, they can be rebuilt based on the scans. CyArk fills their ark with digital copies.

You can download a free, basic program that can make 3D models based on photographs of an object from various angles. The program pieces together the object's surface from the photographs and folds it into a three-dimensional shape.

If you wanted to make a 3D model of the Acropolis, the photographs uploaded to the internet today would suffice, thinks Marble. All those cameras, phones and tablets serve as the internet's eyes in the world.

If she stays where she is, she'll be visible in that day's 3D model as a bulge in the fortification wall.

Scan yourself and send me the file, Daniel wrote when he sent the link.

FROM THE ACROPOLIS'S SOUTH wall, you can see three entrances in the cliffside of Filopappou Hill. The entrances are located next to one another and lead into a small complex of caves known as Socrates's Prison.

In the archives of the Benaki Museum is a photograph from the Second World War showing the entrances to Socrates's Prison sealed off by a thick wall of concrete. A man is leaning against the concrete wall, reading a newspaper.

In the newspaper is a photograph of the Nazis raising their flag atop the Acropolis. Greece is occupied.

Hidden behind the concrete wall are the Acropolis Museum's sculptures, side by side in the dark. The korai are there. They were moved out of the museum under the cover of night, in a reverse archaeological manoeuvre. A burial in the hill. All three entrances are then sealed off by the concrete wall.

Meanwhile, in London, the Parthenon sculptures are removed from the British Museum and hidden in the tunnels of the Underground, in the stretch between Aldwych and Holborn.

The British Museum is bombed during the Blitz the following year.

The Acropolis is not bombed. The Nazis find the Acropolis Museum empty.

The young man ordered to raise the Nazi flag took down the Greek flag, wrapped himself in it and threw himself off the hill. His death was not photographed.

THAT NIGHT IT RAINS so hard Marble is certain something in the sky must have burst. That the night and the rain will go on forever, washing the city into the sea. The flooded streets rush like rivers.

Marble leaves the shelter of the orange trees because the rain is dripping in. She slips in the wet grass of a roundabout and finds herself flat on her back.

She looks up at the sky. The raindrops are illuminated by blue floodlights. They pour from a depthless black sky.

'Daniel?'

'Yes, Maggi?'

'The colours are disappearing. The sculptures are losing their surfaces.'

'Isn't there another surface underneath the colours?'

'Yes, the surface of the stone. But stone is uniform and solid, its surface only gives away its depth. The stone's surface is immaterial.'

'There's no such thing as an immaterial surface, Maggi. Besides, stone also has an age, a story.'

'The story of white sculpture, yes.'

'What story is that?'

'The one that claims that the ancient Greeks were the first to refrain from painting their three-dimensional art. That they were capable of bold, abstract thinking because they were able to look beyond the surface and into the world of ideas. That unpainted marble is a testament to the superiority of Western culture.'

'Who's speaking?'

'Renaissance thinkers. Neoclassicists.'

'They're dead. Why not leave the misinterpreting to them?'

'But antiquity is still white, Daniel.'

'As far as I know, antiquity ended 1,500 years ago.'

'But there's still a peculiar reluctance when it comes to accepting colour in classical sculpture. The first traces of paint were documented during the excavation of Pompeii in the mid-1700s, and the last remaining art historical arguments for a colourless antiquity were debunked more than a hundred years ago. Yet the cultural narrative continues to begin with white sculpture, and only afterwards is colour added, if at all. Colour continues to be kept separate from form. It continues to come as a shock.'

'Does it make any difference whether form and colour are kept separate or not?'

'White sculpture starts to flourish during the Renaissance in the 1500s and onwards, alongside European slave trade and colonialism. I fear that it has served to underpin the notion of the superiority of white skin.'

'How so?'

'Perhaps white marble skin was meant to suggest that all skin colours other than white were painted. That humans are essentially white.'

'Are you saying that marble has inherently racist qualities?'

'No, I'm saying that if European culture is founded upon white marble, then both coloured sculpture and coloured people are fighting an uphill battle in Europe.'

'You do it, too.'

'Do what?'

'Talk about *white* people and *coloured* people as though white is the starting point and colour is an addition, something that is added later.'

'Ah. White sculpture is deeply embedded in our language.'

'Careful you don't end up paranoid, Maggi.'

'There's good reason to be. I had a look at Golden Dawn's website and there was a banner showing Venus de Milo next to an African woodcarving. It's *Entartete Kunst* all over again.'

'But surely the Venus de Milo is invalid proof of Western superiority, given that she was heavily painted?'

'Yes. Just as the Parthenon sculptures are invalid proof. Maybe that's why the colours have been wiped away.'

'Oh, them too?'

'Yes.'

'By who?'

'By archaeologists when they dug up their finds. By art collectors. Cast makers. Conservators at museums. Cleaners. As late as the 1930s they were still cleaning the Parthenon sculptures at the British Museum.'

'To get rid of the colour?'

'The colour was considered part of the filth. The cleaners had the image of white marble in their minds, and they scrubbed using copper tools and ammonia until they could see it. Afterwards, professionals examined the sculptures and found that they did not bear traces of colour.'

Laila,

*Thank you for the letter with the spring leaf from Brooklyn.
I can picture you leaning out of the window to pick it from
a tree on your street. I've attached an infrared photo of it,
pale as a paper cutting.*

*The loneliness of looking into another colour spectrum is
overwhelming. Like being alone in a crowded place.*

*The leaves of trees pale, just like sculptures fade when the
colours disappear. I've taken pictures of euro notes with
the same filter, and they pale just like the leaves. In close-
ups you can see that they're made of cotton; their folds
look like the folds of the korai's drapery.*

*I know you say that a person isn't either estranged or not.
That one is always both. But you can't understand money
by photographing it. Its material is impenetrable.*

I went to a talk about the 'shadow banking system'. Have

you heard of it? It's an unregulated, parallel global banking system consisting of hedge funds that has gradually sucked all global capital out of regulated banks.

The speaker was the owner of a hedge fund, but by his own estimation a discerning and responsible investor. He proposed that Greece allow hedge funds to operate in the country and 'bet' on the country's future.

'Won't that just make the owners of these hedge funds richer?' someone asked.

To begin with, yes, he said. But that would, he explained, prompt something called the 'trickle-down effect'. They must take us for idiots, to come up with a term like that. Such a feeble sound: trickle.

Money rushes through the world, with the internet. Through us and over our heads. I got dizzy and had to go lie down in the institute's courtyard. I looked up at the clouds, and the sky was teeming with what looked like luminous sperm cells. Do you see them, too? Tiny quivering vectors. I wondered whether that's what money is, but I was being silly. They served us hors d'oeuvres and chilled white wine.

Laila, I don't want to be sent into orbit.

I know what you're thinking: Daniel, yes. He can help me stay on Earth, live the life a human is supposed to. All the way down at the surface.

MARBLE

ANNE MARIE BRODERSEN AND Carl Nielsen meet

each other in Paris in the spring of 1891. On the 1st of March, Carl writes in his journal:

Slept well, but awoke with an odd, indeterminable feeling towards morning. Marie Brodersen!

And a few days later:

Cannot recall what I did today apart from this evening, when I saw the woman for whom I have always felt an entire scale of emotions. We shall live our lives together and be happy, and nothing will ever make me doubt it again.

The feeling is mutual. Even though Marie's parents order her to come home right away, she and Carl celebrate their engagement in Paris on the 10th of April before eloping to Italy, where they marry in Florence one month later. She adopts his name like a piece of jewellery, a two-part bronze cast with a sprue in the middle: *Carl-Nielsen.*

Marie writes in her memoirs:

My parents did not believe that a poor artist could support a wife, and indeed, after we returned from our travels, daily life was not too merry. My husband earned 95 kroner per month as a musician in the Royal Orchestra and that was difficult for us to live on. We lived in an attic and were too poor to buy a pram, for instance, when we had children – which we soon did. When the children required fresh air and sunlight, my husband and I would have to carry them through the streets in our arms.

Irmelin was born already in December 1891, Søs in 1893 and Hans Børge in 1895. Ten years pass with children and work. Carl is a violinist at the Royal Danish Theatre and composes on the side, while Marie is a member of The Free Exhibition and shows her work there.

But in the spring of 1903 the children are put into care, paid for with an advance from Carl's music publisher. Carl takes a leave of absence from the theatre and visits Marie in Athens, both of them subsisting on her grant. It's a second honeymoon.

They take the train to Kifissia and hike up Mount Pentelicus to the marble quarry north of the city. There they find a big, beautiful tortoise and bring it with them back to town.

There is an audacity to Marie when it comes to her work. As a young woman, she puts on a red nightgown and rolls around in front of a bull to get it into position. Now the tortoise trots around in the sun on the balcony at the Hotel Achilleion. A few years later she makes a bronze bust with eyes of gold, silver and tortoiseshell.

But perhaps the tortoise is Carl's idea. He is equal parts impetuous and industrious. He grows a moustache and composes a piece about the southern sun, the *Helios Overture*. When he goes for a hike in the mountains and wants to smoke but has forgotten his matches, he asks his friend to light the cigarette with his pistol. Carl holds the cigarette between his lips and inhales while his friend fires at the tip. *After 6 shots we succeeded*, he writes to his friends in Copenhagen, and, *naturally, the tobacco tasted excellent.*

Marie cannot stand idleness. *I long for work*, she writes in her journal already in January. In March she is granted permission to copy the three-headed monster Typhon. Each morning she goes to the museum when it opens. She transfers its form to the clay, recreates its surfaces and fractures. Soon she is the person who has looked at the Typhon the longest and hardest since it was unearthed. It is this intimate knowledge of its shape and surfaces that enables her to see that the archaeologists have made a mistake when assembling the sculpture.

There are no points of contact between the fractured surfaces that the archaeologists could use to guide them. In a letter to a friend, Marie explains that it was *the course of the outer surface* that revealed to her that the Typhon's third head had been incorrectly positioned.

With the museum's blessing, she repositions the head. She turns it and the surfaces fall into place.

DANIEL'S FACE ON THE iPad is life-size and speaks to Marble without delay. The fluid crystals turn their coloured faces in every direction.

He's an image that she can move behind the glass. She can drag him around, enlarge and shrink him.

Are the images located right behind the glass? Or deeper within, like in a shop window? Do our fingers touch the glass the same way our eyes touch the words we read?

'Daniel, did you find me when you searched for images of the Acropolis?'

'Yes, I found you; you were reading in a shell hole in the wall.'

'Yes. I'm stuck.'

'Ah.'

'Won't you come down here and get me?'

Marble and Daniel don't look directly into the camera when they speak. They look at each other on the screen and in doing so they look past each other. As though both are preoccupied by something else, which they are.

By the image of each other.

An eye has a shape: a half-sphere in a hollow. A happy little half-sphere.

You can have a conversation so close to someone else's face that you forget it isn't your own.

You can look at each other and say: I miss you. There are many kinds of absence and presence.

Marble has seen a film about men who have relation-ships with life-size female dolls cast in silicone and develop genuine feelings for them. One man says he's lost the desire to have relationships with 'organic women'. Another demonstrates how he uses the camera's self-timer to take pictures with his silicone-cast girl-friend. In the photo, the two of them are equally alive.

Daniel has seen a film about women who have relation-
ships with objects. Who date them. A bow or a bridge.
The Berlin Wall or the Eiffel Tower. Who press their
warm sex against the Eiffel Tower's cold steel and rejoice.

MARBLE WAKES UP FEELING as though Daniel has just been there. A deep breath passes through the flat: the sound of two workers on the roof of the building across the street, pouring construction debris bucket by bucket through a chute into a skip on the street.

There's a flutter in her stomach muscles that comes from dehydration. A taste of naphthalene in her mouth. There's a dried-out felt-tip pen on her nightstand.

She drinks a glass of water and thinks: So that's that.

The sky is a harsh shade of cyan blue. It could be artificial, but what is an artificial sky? A piece of coloured paper held in front of a lamp? Imagine taking such care, that someone would stand on the horizon somewhere, adjusting the light.

The sun has no arms, no tongues, nothing but current. Colours are asleep at midday. All surfaces are desaturated. You have to navigate by the contours.

A loud sound, and once you hear this sound you realise that the sounds have been sleeping, too. A sheet of iron is dropped into the skip.

Marble carries bananas home in a peach plastic bag. As long as they're in the bag, their colour is preserved. The banana's yellow oilskin peel remembers so well.

She slips on the stairs and comes upon her own nervous system, after the nerves' inherent delay.

The dried mud beneath her soles is a kind of cast, too.

Milk trickles into the sewer. An electric door to a garage rolls up halfway, a woman ducks under and steps outside, stands in front of it and smokes. On the door is a painted sea. Behind the door, an indoor sky. Fluorescent tubes hidden along the stucco.

The mountains have arranged themselves around the city. A cloud grazes a mountain like a hand. An absent-minded caress.

The three-dimensional terrain on Google Earth is a folded image, the same way you can fold a box out of a magazine. There isn't necessarily a connection between the folds and the folded object.

The content of any medium is always another medium, reads Marble. The content of Google Earth is flat photographs taken from above. The content of photographs is the sun's light reflected back from the Earth's surface. The sun sends little parcels of light to Earth. What do the packages contain? Light. What does light contain? Light. The sun is the medium of all media.

Daniel asked what electricity tastes like.

Sulphur? Water? Sun? Marble didn't know.

MARIE TRAVELS BACK TO Athens in November of 1904 to complete her work, this time alone and without a grant, with the hope of earning money off her replicas. She travels via Munich, where the archaeologist Furtwängler shows her a book published by another archaeologist, Wiegand. The book contains images of the Typhon's third head as it was positioned before and as it is positioned now, after she turned it, with no mention of her. She informs Furtwängler that she spent three days repositioning the head, that she paid out of her own pocket for the plasterer who assisted her. That she even has a letter from Wiegand thanking her for the correction.

Das ist ja eine Schändlichkeit und obendrein einer Dame gegenüber, exclaims Furtwängler.

Dame oder nicht Dame, she replies.

She is furious and demands the recognition she deserves.

When she reaches Athens, she works at speed but clashes hard against her surroundings. *By the way, the museums would be fools not to want it*, she writes to Carl regarding one of her copies.

She pulls out her revolver and puts down a sick kitten in the street. Just like Carl, she carries a weapon, but whereas he is brazen, she is considered insane. A group of incensed Greeks hunts her down. With the help of the Danish consulate, she avoids prison and is instead awarded a certificate of honour from the Humane Society.

If only we for once could lead a peaceful, industrious, progressive life together, writes Carl in a letter that December. *But I fear this will never be so. You wish to be a strong man, indeed, preferably to outdo the very strongest of men. Your work and your ambition are so intense, so fervent and beyond all tranquillity or health, and I must say, often I fear that you will break into pieces.*

She writes to him that the Typhon's colours have faded visibly since she last saw it in the summer of 1903, to which he replies: *If everything is constantly changing, there is no need for you to painstakingly copy each and every speck. Remember that!*

But he's mistaken. Her work is urgent. The colours are disappearing.

But the mould-making drags on. The museum's winter opening hours are 10 a.m. to noon and that's hardly enough time for her work. Marie must ask for permission to spend the afternoons in the museum as well, and with the help of a German archaeologist she's granted it.

In January, the copies of the Typhon have all been cast, but Athens is cold and rainy and the plaster is slow to dry. While she waits, Marie starts copying the bull from the same pediment group. *You would not believe what a lovely thing he is*, she writes home to Carl, *his movement is so splendidly dramatic.*

February comes, then March. She copies yet another bull head, a snake and a wing fragment.

Once the plaster is dry, she starts painting her copies. She employs a chemist to help her record and recreate the original colours so she can paint with them. The pigments and methods she uses must correspond to those used in antiquity.

She replicates the traces of colour she can see, meticulously transferring them to the plaster surface.

A few of the copies she paints in vivid colours, as she believes they would have looked when they were made. She does not paint the fractures but leaves them exposed in white plaster.

This is the third head of the Blue-Beard Typhon I have painted, she writes home to her friend Marie Møller. *The beard and hair in a brilliant metallic blue. A bright red face, violet lips, black eyebrows and pupils, and eyes of Spanish green. What more could one want to revel in?*

THE BRIGHT RED MERCURY sulphide known as *cinnabar* was extracted in Istria and Andalusia.

Rust red was made of iron oxides found in the earth.

The same goes for *ochre*.

Yellow and *orange* pigments were extracted in arsenic mines in Anatolia, in modern-day Turkey.

Green malachite and *blue azurite* are copper carbonates that were extracted in silver mines, for example in Laurion, near Athens. Over time, blue azurite may weather and turn into green malachite. Many of the green traces found on sculptures in fact indicate the presence of azure paint.

Even the ancient Egyptians were aware of the transience of blue azurite and produced a more durable synthetic pigment known as *Egyptian blue*: a mixture of lime, quartz sand, copper and natron, which must be heated to 800 degrees Celsius to bond. The Greeks inherited Egyptian blue from the Egyptians.

Tyrian purple was extracted from shells from the Eastern Mediterranean and was worth its own weight in silver.

Black was made of carbon from charred bones and grapevines.

White came from limestone or lead. Women would apply lead to their faces to make themselves paler. White skin was a feminine beauty ideal. Yes, they died of it.

A CHILD IN FRONT of the museum trails after the tourists. She plays a plastic accordion without really playing it. There is a defiance to her movements, and she keeps her hand outstretched when asking for money. She's performing a role, but reluctantly, at a distance from herself. This distance is her tragedy, Marble thinks. She should be in school.

A woman on a bench nearby keeps an eye on the child. Her tragedy is that she is keeping an eye on a child who is earning money.

What does it mean to live illegally? To know that the police can appear at any moment and take you away. To sit, walk, stand and sleep with that knowledge.

Some people here walk hunched over, as though they were

walking on potter's wheels. Some sell umbrellas or sunglasses, depending on the weather. After dark, things that glow. Some gather cardboard or metal in trolleys. Some have very mild eyes, not worn down on rough surfaces.

A man walks by, he wants to record the child playing. He starts filming. She pumps her accordion madly. Then she stops, arms dangling limply at her sides. But the man holds his camera in his left hand and with the index finger of his right he draws circles in the air as though to say: Keep going! I'm filming.

The child starts up again and gives the man what he wants. He's satisfied. He puts the camera away and she extends her hand. He gives her a few coins, but it's not enough and she follows him in the direction of the Acropolis. Intercepts him from one side and then the other. He doesn't give her any more money.

Laila,

I'm in such a terrible mood today, and I'm wondering: is it the economy? Every relation I have here is a trade relation. I go to the museum each morning, I pay for a ticket, buy a cappuccino in the café, give a tip and expect nothing but coffee and courtesy in return. I don't involve myself in anything. Vassilis isn't at the museum at the moment, which suits me just fine. The korai don't recognise me.

I think this non-recognition goes both ways: I don't want to be recognised, and I don't want to recognise. The city is a code I'm not trying to crack. I didn't come to see past the surface. I came to add more surfaces to them. Colour, is what I mean. I'm already very tired of this task.

Now and then, the face of an ancient marble sarcophagus has swollen like a big lump of dough without any features. Do you know why? The sarcophagus is waiting for the deceased, who is also the client. When the client dies, their face is carved into the stone. But every dead person becomes anonymous sooner or later. Don't let the carved faces fool you.

Today, Monday, the museum is closed, so I went to Piraeus for a swim. From the train I saw a gigantic banner with a picture of a spine, and written across it was the word 'scoliosis'. It was a disheartening sight. Something is broken if hospitals are advertising for the illnesses they cure. Although I don't know for sure whether that's what they were doing. There's always this 'don't know', like a bated breath. A man with a little bag that says 'Eye Shop', what did he buy? A girl with the same caricatured features as the doll she holds in her arms as if it were her little sister.

I had to walk for a long time to get to the water, past a harbour with millionaires' yachts the size of mansions, and when I reached the little stretch of dirty beach, three big dogs came racing towards me, growling so viciously I had to return to the road and find a different stairway.

There were people who had errands on the beach; a young man was fishing, and a hunchbacked woman appeared to be searching for something. In the back of a truck parked under a tree lived a family with suntanned skin. Two sunbathers were sitting at a beach café called Blue Lagoon. There was rubbish everywhere. And hovering above the beach, up by the road, was a fancy café that hadn't yet opened, perhaps waiting for the dark hours where a beach like that can seem romantic.

91

I took off my shoes and socks and waded out into the water and thought: I'm going to drown. But I didn't drown. I got back out and sat down at the bus stop to wait for the bus home and shuddered at the sight of a peeling picnic table in front of a café on the other side of the road.

I told myself: Calm down. It's not all business. Life happens here, too.

Here, much of life is lived outside. It's the good weather. What do you want, Marble? For everyone to climb into their coffins right now and hold their breath? Is that what you want?

M

IN THE 1820s, ENGLISHMAN John Deane rescues horses from a burning stable filled with smoke by putting an old barrel helm on his head and pumping air in through a fire hose. In the following years, he and his brother design first a smoke helmet and then a waterproof model that can be attached to a full-body suit made of thick canvas. The helmet and suit make it possible to walk around on the ocean floor, breathing oxygen supplied through a hose. Two men operate an oxygen pump from a boat up at the surface.

The diving suit goes into production in England in the mid-1800s and is introduced to the Greek islands in the 1870s. At the bottom of the Mediterranean grow sponges that can be processed and used in the home. Before the diving suit, the Greeks would free-dive to collect sponges, but with the introduction of the diving suit, areas of the ocean floor at depths of up to 70 metres become accessible. In just a few decades, Greek sponge diving is industrialised.

The sponge diver's work is like a simple computer game: collect sponges, earn points. The diving helmet has four round viewports made of glass, the biggest one in front, and three smaller ones allowing the diver to look up, to the right and to the left. It's dark on the ocean floor. The diver walks against the current, leaning his body forwards as if against a strong wind. He fills his net with ripe sponges and tugs at the rope.

IT'S THE SOUND OF the demonstration pressing its way through the streets, its rhythm and shouts that frighten Marble. She's on Syntagma Square, keeping her distance from the police who await the crowds with batons, helmets, visors, shields, shin guards and machine guns, in long, tight chains. She's waiting, too.

You can't approach a demonstration from the front. You have to slip in from the side or from behind. If it's coming towards you, you have to make yourself flat, step aside.

Marble doesn't want to get caught between the police and the protestors. She scouts for escape routes, sees them open and close around her. She doesn't want to get beaten up and she doesn't want to go to prison.

Now the protestors reach the square, they're carrying banners and signs; a precipice of unknown symbols. A young man wearing a T-shirt with the words *Looking beyond the surface of things* walks past and she joins in, leaving behind the potential escape routes. She glides effortlessly up the hill leading to the parliament, as if walking with a thousand feet. An airiness inside her head.

But then they reach Amalias and see that the police have

blocked off the road. It's wide and empty, like a runway at a remote airport. She can't keep her legs from veering off and leaving the protest.

Behind her the shouts continue, everything continues. In the rest of the city, time stands still. A bird is singing on the fence surrounding the National Garden. A smell of wild rosemary at the entrance.

The National Garden is deserted. All the benches are empty. The sloped seats of ancient marble chairs collect rainwater.

Last time she was here, the park was a labyrinth of meandering paths. A cool, green oasis. Once you get to know a place like this it becomes almost transparent. Cultivated. In a little zoo at the rear of the park there are cages with mountain goats, rabbits and peacocks. An aviary with parrots and budgies. Far too many turtles in a fenced-in pond. *Set them free*, it says on a bench next to the pond.

The park is a preserve and she's alone with the animals. Alone with the signs on the trees. Several of the palms have died. Some have a broad metal band wrapped around their trunk.

She stops at the backside of the parliament, sees that the exit here is blocked. There are shouts and sirens from the other side of the fence. The protest is still going. Now there's singing from a loudspeaker. The crowd claps.

Marble sees a woman on the path up ahead. She's walking beside a large duck, it isn't on a lead. Marble slows down as she gets closer so as not to scare the bird away. The woman says something in Greek, smiles and repeats it in English.

'We're looking for worms,' she says. 'He just found a big one and now he's excited, he wants more.'

She's young, she looks friendly, she has an open face. Marble smiles and wishes them luck. As she walks past, the woman points at the ground somewhere in front of the duck and speaks to it.

Marble stops to photograph a moss-covered fountain at the end of the path. The moss glows in the infrared picture. Floating in the fountain are mushrooms, or perhaps they're knobby fruits. They're the size and shape of a human brain.

'WHICH IS BIGGER, THE real or the virtual?' asks Marble.

'The virtual is the multitude of potentialities in the world,' says the 3D animator. 'It's infinitely detailed and infinitely variable.'

'Is there any limit to the virtual?'

'The limit is beyond human comprehension.'

'So it's humanity itself that constitutes the limit?'

'Only to its own comprehension.'

'Will you help me make a cast in the 3D program?'

'I can't. Nothing solid, fluid or ethereal.'

'Is that the limit to the virtual?'

'The program consists of zeros and ones and light on a screen. That isn't "the virtual".'

'Can the program simulate the making of a cast?'

'Simulate, yes, but is that what you want?'

'Yes.'

'Okay. What would you like?'

'I'd like liquid marble. It was liquid once, and it can become liquid again. And then we can use it to cast.'

'Frozen waves of marble?'

'A tree, a book, a declaration of love.'

'Right. I'll get back to you.'

LINING THE BORDER BETWEEN garden and cloister in the courtyard of the Archaeology Museum is a row of marble sculptures. Their surfaces are severely damaged in parts. Faces, hands, entire fronts and backs have weathered away while other parts of the same sculptures remain as pristine as when they were carved.

Marble assumes it must be their placement and many years of rain that have caused the sculptures to partially disintegrate. Then she takes a closer look at one of them and sees that the damaged areas are riddled with tiny holes and tunnels, like wood attacked by woodworms. On the sculpture's chest a piece of the weathered surface has chipped off, revealing the tightly woven tissue of a coral reef within.

Laila,

I've been reading about Greek sponge divers and the strains under which they worked. In addition to the financial strain (the divers were paid for piecework), the physical (hard labour under pressure on the ocean floor) and the social (internal competition), there was the fear of decompression sickness. Decompression sickness is a phenomenon that arose with the diver's suit. In just decades it killed tens of thousands of Greek divers and incapacitated many more.

You probably know that decompression sickness occurs when the pressure around the body changes too quickly and too frequently, causing bubbles of nitrogen to form in the blood, but the sponge divers didn't. Scientists only discovered it in the late 1800s, and their research was based on the sponge divers' data.

The sponge divers had their own theories and ineffectual methods. The cigarette test, for example. The first thing a diver did after a dive was to smoke a cigarette on deck. Based on the smell of the smoke, a crewmember could tell whether the diver had decompression sickness before the diver showed any symptoms. If the smoke smelled wrong, the diver's skin would soon begin to itch. Severe joint pain, cramps and paralysis could follow. The crew would massage the diver's body to stimulate blood flow. If his condition worsened, they would drop him off on the nearest beach and bury him in hot sand up to his neck. The sand bath relieved the pain but it did not cure.

Decompression sickness is the result of a change to the body's material while its exterior form remains the same – a kind of fatal casting. Under pressure, the air's natural content of nitrogen becomes liquid and can be absorbed into the diver's blood. When the diver then ascends, nitrogen converts back into a gas, expanding and creating bubbles in the blood that get caught in the veins, joints and organs. The mould bursts.

Laila, I long for things to turn into signs, and for signs to turn into objects. To see meaning and materiality collapse into one and the same plane. To creep inside a colour, to live there.

Write soon. I'm afraid I'm developing a form of decompression sickness.

M

CARL IS IMPATIENT, HE grows more desperate each day. He has no appetite, one moment he composes, the next he finds it impossible. He cannot understand why his wife has now been copying Archaic sculptures in Athens for five months.

We shall do it ourselves, my dear! he writes, and *Look, we await you with cymbals and kettledrums! And we will trumpet your name as the very greatest, and you too shall become a great artist.*

And in February: *You, capable of such composition and so full of ideas, and yet you waste your days as a copyist in a museum. Perhaps it pays a paltry sum, but you are wasting your best and most prolific years and the measly honour gained is worth nothing at all. Perhaps a few archaeologists and that sort will acknowledge it, but no one else.*

It is said that an archaeological excavation is a recreation of the time and place it uncovers. In the same way, perhaps when Marie is at the museum she cannot tell the difference between original and copy. They're two identically folded surfaces with lines of time extending between them. When Marie follows the surface's folds with her hands and tools, she moves along these lines, back and forth.

The Bull's Head you learned from, of course, so that is well and good, writes Carl, *but the Typhon? It is hardly amusing in the long run; I mean pure, real, alive, truly artistic. Its form is too silly, in my opinion.*

Carl can't understand why Marie would choose the Archaic over the Classical. Why she looks further back than renowned sculptors like Bertel Thorvaldsen did, for example, seeking out the imperfect, expressive sculpture of the Archaic period. Why it matters that the sculptures are coloured, and that the colour is gaudy and saturated.

Carl asks her to produce *big, brilliant, autonomous works*. He does not understand that the classical ideal has been exhausted.

Marie's work is not modern, but it does hint at it. Her preoccupation with the Archaic is not unlike the Fauves' preoccupation with African art a few years later.

The tone of their correspondence sharpens at the end of February when Carl has his premiere of his choral work *The Sleep*.

On the 18th of February Carl writes:

I was looking at the photograph yesterday and it baffles me that you did not finish at least a month ago. The Typhon was far enough along to be photographed two years ago. Now you write that the colour is causing you trouble!!!

And later, in the same letter: *But do as you like, our relationship which was once loving and genuine – on my part, at least – has gone to the dogs as it is.*

Marie responds on 28 February:

Unfortunately, the colours are no quick ordeal, and I should think it unnecessary to tell you that I am not idly waiting, and that I cannot again leave it all behind, you yourself would ridicule me for that, and so if I am to make progress, I must complete my work and stay where I am.

It grieves me not to attend the premiere of your choral work, but so it seems to be for us this year. You could not come to Ribe for my celebration and now I cannot come to your Sleep.

A few days before, Carl has written:

We never hear from you! I received a tattered postcard the other day in which you wrote that you had now left your plaster things to dry on a heater. You should have thought of that from the beginning. Have you not been experimenting with paint on smaller pieces of plaster all this time you have been waiting for the Typhon to dry? I would have thought that obvious.

On the 4th of March, Marie replies:

I think it is rare for a man to respect his wife's work. How can you sit in Copenhagen dictating how I am to cut my models and leave them to dry? Unfortunately, what I left on the heater is now partly ruined. And now this intolerable ordering me about on my trip and criticism with no regard whatsoever for my own thinking, treating me as if I were a little boy, a child in need of a spanking.

The post they send on a Tuesday arrives the following Sunday, meaning it takes ten days after sending a letter for a reply to come. It is this delay their correspondence is up against. The desperation in Carl's letters grows after he's fired from the Royal Theatre at the beginning of March, and he concludes a letter:

But what now? If you with your fortune and your income would support yourself and the children, I could start over abroad. Or what do you think?

Marie has not yet received the letter and writes: *That bloody theatre*, all that double-crossing, isn't he glad to be rid of it, couldn't he come visit her?

In a letter dated the 23rd of March, he replies:

I was deeply distressed to receive such a letter from you today. Knowing that I have just been dismissed, you ask me to travel to Athens or meet you in Rome and then to travel home over Paris!!! What are you thinking? I have wept bitterly and I am certain you must have lost your mind and that I too have gone mad.

And later on in the same letter: *All I ask is that we now get our*

107

divorce over and done with. It is greatly distressing to announce this to you, and I care for you so deeply, and it will be difficult, indeed, terrible to be without the children. But it must be so. Then I shall start a whole new life and leave the past behind me.

Marie sends a telegram as soon as she receives the letter:

My dear Carl / Come immediately / Bring money / Your girl does not want a divorce

'NO CAST WAS EVER made of Anne Marie Carl-Nielsen's face,' says Marble. 'She cast Holger Drachmann's face and right hand after his death in 1908, she made Sophus Claussen's death mask in 1931 and Carl's in October that year and in her later years she even made a cast of her own left hand, but no one ever made a cast of her face, neither dead nor alive. So if we want to recreate her in 3D, we'll have to do so using photographs.'

'Do we have any?' asks the 3D animator.

'Plenty,' replies Marble. 'She was deliberate about having her picture taken with her most important works before they left the studio.'

Marble flips through a book and points to photographs of Anne Marie Carl-Nielsen. One in front of the Typhon at the Acropolis Museum in June 1903. One in a smock and black turban in front of a marble bust; it's Carl, she's holding a chisel to his throat.

'The scenario is staged,' says Marble. 'She never learned to carve marble. The model was sent to Carrara and carved there instead.'

Marble flips ahead and points to a photograph of Marie in a white men's suit standing atop the back of a plaster cast of Christian IX's equestrian statue. And one of the entire team in front of the completed statue at bronze founder Rasmussen's workshop. One of her on a ladder beside the Carl Nielsen Monument in plaster, a sculpture of Pan on a wild horse that was meant to have wings. One behind the plaster model of the Mermaid with fish-like features and a mighty, tucked-under tail. One of her at work once again on a small animal model, a lying cow. One of her, blurry, next to the enormous sculpture of Jutland's Stallion, the Chieftain.

'This is the last photograph taken of her,' says Marble. 'She had an assistant cover the Chieftain with wet rags because she intended to continue her work as soon as she recovered. When she died, the clay dried up; the sculpture crumbled and was discarded.'

There are also portraits of Marie at various ages with her hair pinned up and parted down the middle. She looks directly into the camera with a clear, firm gaze.

'Do you think we can recreate her in 3D based on the photographs I've shown you?' asks Marble. 'And can we animate her?'

'You don't have any pictures of her from behind?'

'No.'

'It will be difficult to recreate her backside.'

'The back isn't so important. Her face is what matters. Can you combine the images and make her speak?'

'Yes, but it'll be in greyscale and pieced together from many different points in time.'

'I'd like to see her the way she looked on the 28th of March 1905, when she sends a telegram to Carl to say that she doesn't want a divorce and asking him to come. She's 41 then.'

'I'll do my best. Did he come?'

'Who?'

'Carl. Or did they divorce?'

'She wrote a letter the same night asking him again to come. We know from bookkeeping records that they exchanged telegrams over the following days. The telegrams weren't saved. But on the 1st of April, she stopped working and left Athens.'

'She went home?'

'Yes. And returned in May to paint and sell the final copies of the Typhon and the Bull's Head. Their marriage was saved. But she promised Carl not to make any more copies.'

MARBLE PUTS ON BLACK leggings, a black windbreaker, black trainers and sunglasses, pulls her hair into a pony-tail and breezes through the city with long strides.

She passes the cats by the fence but doesn't take notice

of them. She's on her way to a yoga class at the foot of the Acropolis.

The yoga teacher's hands are eager when he asks her how old she is and pushes her hips deeper into the pose. A silverfish twinkles on one of his ears. The body as the grave of the soul, who was it who said that?

He tells the yoga class to close their eyes and imagine their eyeballs dropping back into their heads.

'Like two stones sinking to the bottom of a lake.'

Her eyes sink to the bottom of the lake and roam restlessly about. Bodies leaf through poses. All the city's statues: bodies of bronze, wood, marble. Bodies of flesh and bone on yoga mats; long, taut tendons. The names of poses: the Discus Thrower, the Sander, the Boxer, the Clown, the Lion, the Cobra, the Warrior.

When Marble opens her eyes, the people on the mats around her have been replaced by painted sculptures. Vividly executed with inlaid eyes of crystal. Jewellery in precious metals. Clothing in rich earth tones. Their skin is waxen, dyed. No one breathes.

Yoga is a series of unmoving poses. How can a human turn into stone? Stand in the shape of a tree or mountain, fossilised?

Marble assumes the mountain pose. She plants the soles of her feet firmly on the mat and lets her arms hang along her sides, palms facing forwards. At first she

113

sways, but then something inside her contracts. Hardens. A cool weight. Her heart slows and beats like drift ice. Her face sinks inwards.

Visual time has ceased. Her eyes don't move. Whiteout and then: no signal. Not even black or white.

What does it mean to be stone? To be Marble, as in made of marble? She is the same thing the whole way through. Uniform. Solid.

The solid as an ascent to the surface. She is her surface to the core.

She feels a warm hand, a human touch. The yoga teacher. There's no need to react.

She doesn't fall asleep, she doesn't dream. There are images before her eyes. They come from within, outside of time.

Weightless images of Saint Petersburg in May. The Summer Garden's slender trunks against a light night sky. The churches' columns overlaid with smooth porphyry.

The imitated, the clad, the gilded.

'Is the gold solid or gilded?' asks a voice.

'It's gilded,' answers another. 'Don't be silly. Stop scratching at the surfaces. Don't kiss the lips of the deceased, everything about them is dead.'

'The green marble is painted on,' whispers a third. 'The

floor mosaic is made of hardwood. The woodcarvings are made of wood-coloured stone.'

'A window to a viewing garden looks like a door,' says the other, 'but don't jump through. The metro's escalator continues downwards, but not forever. It isn't the white nights but artificial daylight that glows beneath the steps.'

'Palaces reek of mould,' says the first.

'Little monkeys in costumes sit on the shoulders of men who dream of money.'

'The colours on the surface of the petrol leaking into the canal can only be seen from certain angles,' whispers the third voice.

'Maggi,' says a fourth.

'All dreams are slippery,' says the first. 'A tiny red velvet cushion crawls across the path. If you look carefully at the sun while it sets, you can feel it slipping.'

'You aren't solid,' says the fourth.

It's a soft voice, a voice she knows. Daniel. She has to answer.

The reply takes form from the outside first; it starts as a slight tremor all across her surface and rises towards her throat, enters her vocal chords, tunes them, makes them vibrate. The sound is mechanical.

'Da-ni-el.'

And then more fluently:

'Are you coming?'

Then her body is on the yoga mat once more, full of blood.

Heavy as a statue toppling to the ground.

Athens 28.3.1905   *Tuesday night*

Carl, my own dear boy.

My knees feel as though they are broken, late this evening I staggered to the post office to telegraph and once there I could not think.

I have been sitting on pins and needles awaiting your letter to hear how the hymn went. The evening of the performance I was so anxious I nearly caused a scandal, and I sat with the clock calculating Greek and European time down to the minute. Afterwards I waited for a telegram which did not come; and then tonight I received your letter.

I must tell you plainly I do not want to divorce, for the simple reason that you are most dear to me.

Now you must *travel down and bring me home, it will do you good in the wake of that horrible theatre ordeal, over which you should not fret. The two of us will manage, sometimes you will earn money, sometimes I. I am convinced that it is better for you not to be associated with that insidious theatre where mediocrity reigns. Your time will come –*

Where should I start my head is aching my entire body is freezing, it is starting to grow light. How horrible we humans can be to one another, and often without meaning to.

If only I could tuck my head under your shirt, just a moment under your shirt, instead of sitting here at dawn soaking a hotel sofa with my tears.

Granted, I love my work, but it is no immoral love and in truth I have more flesh and blood than most, but I often hide. My poor boy. My wish for you to come is no foolish whim, financially I will earn the money back with my dear Typhon and my lovely Bull, but until I hear back from you my arms may as well be broken above the elbow. –

I write this letter with despair, knowing that you will not receive it for another 5 days.

The last letter you refer to had been written before I received your letter regarding the dismissal which honestly does not surprise me nor sadden me all that much, we will manage so long as we are good to one another. Now I imagine myself wrapping my arms around you and resting my head against your chest and listening to your anxious little heart beating, can you feel it?

Come and be my good, dearest boy and in good heart.

SHE PICKS UP DANIEL at the metro, he arrives from the airport, it's the week before Easter. She puts on a black dress and a wristwatch, ties her hair up into a bun. She assumes a soft, relaxed pose in front of the mirror.

119

'My darling,' she whispers to her reflection.

'My darling,' she whispers while she waits at the metro. She doesn't recognise him. She sees a man in a beige trench coat walking towards her, he smiles, he speaks with Daniel's voice. Is it Daniel? He seems to recognise her.

Has she stared at too many carved marble faces to recognise a living one? Is a smile or a raised eyebrow all it takes for a face to come loose and fall away like tissue paper around an orange?

Can you love a man in a trench coat, she also wonders. But he tastes of tobacco and aniseed when they kiss.

This assemblage of atoms. This cloud of facial expressions. The taste of boiled sweets. Yes, she'll call it Daniel.

'Daniel.'

Marble and Daniel circle the Acropolis and each other like moons around planets. Her blood is circulating once again. A sun shines in Athens that can shine right through them. They're nourished, the way people are nourished by light. By seeing each other illuminated in a whole new way.

Like the pictures you see through your eyelids when you lie on your back in the sun.

They put mattresses on the floor and open the balcony door. The door's white curtain is a horizontal extension of the bed sheets. The sounds of the room and the sounds of the street pass through the curtain from opposite sides.

Everything is fluid beneath a sun like this. The sheets are stained like used cloth napkins. When they squeeze lemon onto apples, the peels lose their colour.

Baked inside the baker's Easter bread is a red egg; the egg was dyed when it was boiled. The oven's heat adds a layer of blue around the yolk. Marble picks out the egg and cuts the bread into slices.

She tells Daniel about the golden death mask she saw in the Prehistoric Gallery at the Archaeological Museum. A thin sheet of gold pressed across the face of the deceased. Metal protecting a form it was given more than 3,000 years ago.

Daniel's eyes shine like translucent glass. Sunlight pierces one eye from the side, lighting up its blue like an illuminated swimming pool in a place where steam rises from the water at night.

If there is a desire, it is the legs' desire to become mineral. And the head's desire to become weightless and internal. Their bodies are pulled in both directions. In the middle the sexes wrap around each other, wet like two hands washing.

IN OCTOBER 1900 A Greek sponge diving boat is returning from the coast of Africa, where its divers have gathered sponges all season long. Piled up on deck and hanging from the railings are big nets stuffed with cleaned, bleached and squeezed sponges.

Off the Greek island of Antikythera, the ship encounters a storm and the captain decides to drop anchor and wait for it to pass. In the meantime, the divers are sent out to look for more sponges.

They gather sponges at a depth of 60 metres. No one has ever dived this deep in the area before. They fill one net and then another, tug at the rope when they're ready to be pulled up.

One of the divers signals to be pulled up early; he tugs hard at his lifeline. When they take off his helmet, his face is pale. He tells them he's seen a pile of corpses on the seabed below the ship: the decomposing bodies of horses and humans.

The captain comes out on deck and the diver repeats what he saw. The captain assumes a lack of oxygen or divers' disease must have made the diver delusional, but he decides to take a look himself. He puts on his diving gear and jumps into the water.

At the bottom the captain sees something quite different from what the sponge diver saw. He sees the remnants of an ancient Greek shipwreck carrying precious cargo: ancient marble and bronze sculptures half-buried in the seafloor.

The captain is right. The ship is a Roman ship that sank in the first century BC, loaded with art and handicrafts plundered in Greece shortly before the wreck. The horses have hides of bronze, the humans have skin of marble.

The majority of the cargo is salvaged in autumn of 1900 and spring of 1901. Throughout the process, the divers cannot shake the feeling of pulling petrified corpses out of the sea.

The salvaging work is suspended when a diver ascends too quickly and dies of what we know today is decompression sickness.

The salvaged marble sculptures are installed at the Archaeological Museum in Athens, along the cloister in the courtyard.

The parts of the marble sculptures that protruded from the seabed for 2,000 years were corroded by corals and marine life. Half and whole faces, parts of arms, chests and backs have disintegrated into coral-like structures.

Meanwhile, the parts of the marble sculptures that were buried in the seabed are well preserved. Hands, faces, feet and halves of backs remain as they were when originally carved. A buttock, a thigh, a calf, soft skin, incised hair.

Each sculpture possesses both types of surface, marble skin and corroded coral structure, with sharp transitions in between.

'BY THE WAY, THE liquid marble – I think I've found a solution,' says the 3D animator.

'What?' asks Marble.

'The translucency is what's been causing me trouble. Light travels quite some ways into marble before it's reflected. If you don't take that into account, marble ends up looking like plaster.'

'Victorian marble.'

'Exactly, it looks lifeless. Here I've put two layers on top of each other and made the outer layer semi-translucent. Light is reflected in the inner layer and cast back through the outer layer. If you want more layers, let me know.'

'It looks good. But how do you make it liquid?'

'That's easy. Under "properties" is a setting called "liquid". You select the object, click "liquid" and it turns fluid. I set the elasticity low to make it thicker. How thick do you want it?'

'Like water.'

'Or milk?'

'Yes.'

'OK. I've got something else to show you, too.'

A face appears on the screen.

'Marie?'

'Yes.'

'Can she talk?'

'She can move her mouth, but she's missing a voice.'

'No problem. That isn't necessary. I've planned a voice-over with several voices. A conversation.'

'I'll let you handle that. Should we do the recordings now?'

'Yes. How does it work? Do you do a screen recording?'

'No, you insert a virtual camera in the 3D space and preset its movements.'

'And how the objects should move relative to each other?'

'Yes.'

'And then we record a film using the virtual camera?'

'Then the camera prints a bunch of stills in high resolution, which are played in succession to create a film. Afterwards, you can add sound.'

MARBLE AND DANIEL TAKE the train to Kifissia at the northern end of the city and then a taxi to the marble quarry. Mr Manolis from Dionysso Marble picks them up at the entrance in a red Toyota Corolla. He has a stiff leg, perhaps as a result of polio.

Marble and Daniel climb into the back seat. Mr Manolis offers them cigarettes from a gold-plated case and they smoke in the car as they drive up a winding road, past the marble sawmill and straight into the quarry.

'Oh,' they exclaim when an immense valley full of white cubes opens up before them. They roll down their windows and the smoke is sucked from the car out into the valley.

The quarry looks like a building carved into the mountain-side, with a staircase leading up to three big doors. But

128

when they get closer, they see that the scale is off. The stairway's steps are at least five metres tall, the doors triple that.

Mr Manolis parks the car on one of the gigantic steps that have been hewn into the mountain. The three of them climb out of the car.

'There was once a coral reef here,' says Mr Manolis.

He's a geologist.

'Here?'

'Yes. Marble consists of ancient corals and shellfish that have been compressed at high pressures and temperatures until they become crystalline; *calcite*.'

He stamps on the rock with his stiff leg.

'Coral is an animal, not a plant. It consists of thousands of tiny polyps that form a shared external skeleton across generations.'

'Yes,' says Marble. 'We're standing on the flattened skeleton of one gigantic dead organism.'

'The rock isn't dead,' says Mr Manolis.

'Not dead?'

'No. The coral's common skeleton survives the replacement of one generation by the next. We call this common life form *mineral*. Mineral life can't be crushed to death the way biological life can. Mineral life is always both living and dead.'

'Immortal?'

'Beyond the distinction between life and death.'

'We're standing on a mineral form of collective dead life that is still lived while dead,' says Daniel.

'Or life that's deadened,' says Marble, and adds, looking at Daniel: 'So the sponge diver was right about the coral-eaten sculptures after all.'

'About them not being dead?' asks Daniel.

'Yes, and not alive either,' says Marble.

'The words are a little too narrow,' says Mr Manolis. 'We call it marble. And our job is to cut it into pieces.'

Mr Manolis points down at a small round hole in the rock next to the Corolla.

'We drill two holes, one vertical and one horizontal, and when the two meet somewhere inside the rock, we pull a diamond chainsaw through and let it run for days and days. You can see one in action down there.'

Marble and Daniel peer over the edge and feel dizzy. A big machine on caterpillar tracks is sawing at the very slab they're standing on.

'We do that from three sides, which gives us a cube. Let's say it's six by six by nine metres. That's 324 cubic metres of solid crystalline structure. 880 tonnes.'

Mr Manolis walks back to the car.

'Even in antiquity they were able to carve out suitable slabs and transport them. The Parthenon is built of marble from this quarry. Hop back in and I'll show you the sawmill.'

The sawmill is electric. A slew of machines are sawing slabs of various shapes and sizes.

'The marble and blade can overheat,' says Mr Manolis as the car creeps past the sawmill, which is working away in the sun. 'That's why you need water when you saw. It makes the marble glisten and spray like fountains. The water leads the dust away, and it collects as white residue in drains and gutters.'

He tells Marble and Daniel to open up the door on either side of the car.

'There's the white water, running right beneath us,' says Marble.

'The dust is collected and sold as animal feed,' says Mr Manolis.

'As calcium supplements?' asks Daniel, closing his door again.

'Yes,' answers Mr Manolis.

'Oh,' whispers Marble. 'Animals have bones made of mountains. That's the force keeping them upright.'

Then she topples sideways out of the open car door and rolls to the roadside. Mr Manolis stops the car and he and Daniel leap out and run back.

They find her in a ditch with white water trickling across her. Frozen on her lips is an Archaic smile.

LAILA:
The surface is where an object ends and perception begins. It's both materiality and idea, not either-or.

MARBLE:
Surfaces are what I long for.

THE 3D ANIMATOR:
Painted plaster copies?

DANIEL:
Imagine that the surface of the body continues inwards the way it does with a solid marble sculpture. That you cut into me and inside there is nothing but skin.

MARBLE:
Like cutting into marzipan.

LAILA:
White sculpture is an aspect of decomposition, not an antique ideal per se.

VASSILIS:
It was time and oblivion that made the sculptures white.

Later on, 'renaissance' and misinterpretation.

MARBLE:
And ammonia and copper utensils.

THE 3D ANIMATOR:
Is Western culture founded upon a misinterpretation?

LAILA:
It's founded upon its own demise.

KORE:
(laughter)

VASSILIS:
The heads and hands of Acrolithic sculpture were made of marble while the bodies were wooden skeletons draped in fabric.

MARBLE:
So much for the solid marble body.

VASSILIS:
The korai's outstretched arms are attachments. And the tips of their hair that lift from their chest, they're attached too.

KORE:
Our fractures are intrinsic.

MARBLE:
Both colour and fractures should be considered part of the form.

LAILA:
Could form be considered folded surfaces?

MR MANOLIS:
Even marble consists of unfathomable amounts of surfaces folded into one another.

DANIEL:
Surfaces present images the way screens do.

LAILA:
Vision and touch are wound together like fibres in a rope.

THE DIVER:
To prove that the diving suit wasn't dangerous, the seller had his pregnant wife dive off the quay in it.

DANIEL:
I found her half-buried in the seabed.

MARBLE:
I saw my own face in the mirror as a reconstruction of something lost long ago.

VASSILIS:
Remnants of leaf gold were found on top of the paint.

THE 3D ANIMATOR:
Do you want the liquid marble to change colour?

DANIEL:
The cigarette smoke smells strange.

MARBLE:
What do you do with reciprocated love?

DANIEL:
Can you cast it and make it solid?

MARBLE:
Airport security asked me to remove the cap so they could look into the camera through the lens.

THE CAT:
The sun is a hole in the sky.

THE 3D ANIMATOR:
It's possible to reconstruct a person's face based on the DNA in a strand of hair, but you can't reconstruct their age.

MARBLE:
DNA has no age.

MARIE:
Come and I will be strong and the Typhon and I will pay for the trip Remember to reserve a bunk Travel is inexpensive right now.

DANIEL:
Today I saw the sun's journey etched across the sky like the path of an arrow, and I thought, the sun is something we lend to other days.

MARBLE:
Now heavy, luminous drops of rain have started to fall.

VASSILIS:
The sculptures are headed for a future without surfaces. A future of air and running water. Beneath a white rainbow.

DANIEL:
The sponge divers are dancing on the harbour, Maggi. Want to come along and see?

MARBLE:
Yes, in a bit.

MR MANOLIS:
Humanity will not exist long enough to discover traces of its culture as sediment in marble.

KORE:
We must allow the air to touch still more surfaces.

VASSILIS:
Bronze can be melted and reused.

DANIEL:
When you love, it's the face of the beloved you see, whether you're happy or miserable.

KORE:
Is love a fold of the heart?

MARIE:
Things accumulate, they don't disappear.

NOW A FACE EMERGES from a landscape of steam. A woman's face with her hair parted down the middle and tied into a bun on top of her head. She has a round chin, narrow eyes and lips. An open, unclouded gaze. It's Marie.

At the very bottom of the steam landscape, far below Marie's face, is a sea of marble. The camera tilts downwards and dives until it's just a few metres above the marble sea. Hovering above the sea is a mould, it looks like a big egg made of plaster. At the top of the mould is a hole.

Marie's face has followed the camera down to the surface of the sea. A left hand, Marie's, forms a cup and scoops up some of the marble sea. She pours it into the mould through the hole at the top. Carefully she sets down the mould and lets it float on the surface.

The mould cracks open and a diver with a helmet appears within. He fastens the helmet to his diving suit and jumps into the sea.

Marie watches the circular marble ripples that spread from where the diver jumped in. She turns her side to the camera; her face is backless, like a mask.

The camera follows the diver's air hose down into the depths. The marble sea isn't solid – you can see the diver as soon as the camera breaks through the surface.

He kneels down on the seabed beside a sculpture he's unearthing.

Surrounding the diver and the sculpture is a coral reef, shimmering in every shade of the rainbow.

The camera zooms in on the sculpture. It's a 3D scan of a kore. The kore's surface is pieced together from Marble's infrared photographs and folded into a three-dimensional form. Where data is missing, the sculpture has holes. Through the holes, you can see inside the sculpture. Both interior and exterior are made up of the same magenta image of the kore's surface.

The camera zooms back out. The diver ties his lifeline around the kore and signals to be pulled up to the surface.

The camera remains on the seabed.

IMAGE APPENDIX

A.   Anne Marie Carl-Nielsen photographed by Mary Steen, 1883.
© Carl Nielsen Museum/Odense City Museums

B.   *A Calf Licking Itself* and *A Calf Scratching Itself Behind Its Ear*, bronze sculptures, Anne Marie Carl-Nielsen, 1888.
© National Gallery of Denmark/
Jakob Skou-Hansen

C.   Anne Marie Carl-Nielsen and Carl Nielsen at the Acropolis Museum in front of Anne Marie Carl-Nielsen's copy of the Typhon, postcard 1903.
© Carl Nielsen Museum/Odense City Museums

D.   Section of frieze intended for the pediment of Christian IX's equestrian statue, clay model, Anne Marie Carl-Nielsen, 1909.
© Carl Nielsen Museum/Odense City Museums

E.   Copper tools used for cleaning the Parthenon sculptures in 1937-38.
© Trustees of the British Museum

F.   Socrates's Prison, photographed by Dimitris Harissiadis, 1947.
© Benaki Museum Athens

G.   Section of a 5-euro note, infrared photograph, 2013.

H.   Acr. 676, 3D model, 2013.

A

B

C

D

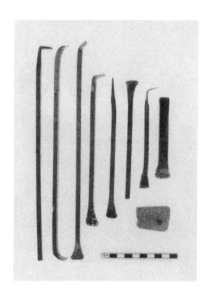

E

F

G

H

Biographies

Amalie Smith (b. 1985) is a Danish writer and visual artist. A graduate from the Danish Academy of Creative Writing and the Royal Danish Academy of Fine Arts, Smith has published eight hybrid books. She has received numerous awards for her work as an artist and writer, including the Danish Arts Foundation's prestigious three-year working grant, the Danish Crown Prince Couple's Rising Star Award, and the Bodil and Jørgen Munch-Christensen Prize for emerging writers.

Jennifer Russell has published translations of Christel Wiinblad and Peter-Clement Woetmann, and in 2019 she received the Gulf Coast Prize for her translation of Ursula Scavenius's 'Birdland'.

Marble
Copyright © Amalie Smith, 2014
Published by agreement with Copenhagen Literary Agency ApS,
Copenhagen
Translation copyright © Jennifer Russell, 2020
This English translation first published in the United Kingdom
by Lolli Editions in 2020
Second edition, 2022

The right of Amalie Smith to be identified as the author of this work
has been asserted in accordance with Section 77 of the Copyright,
Designs and Patents Act 1988

Marble is No. 4 in the series New Scandinavian Literature

Graphic design by Ard – Chuard & Nørregaard
Cover typeset in LL Medium (Robert Huber/Lineto)
Text typeset in Media77
Printed and bound by TJ Books in Cornwall, United Kingdom, 2022

KONSUL GEORGE IORCK OG
HUSTRU EMMA JORCK'S FOND

This translation was made possible through the generous support of the
Danish Arts Foundation, the Carl Nielsen and Anne Marie Carl-Nielsen
Foundation, and the Konsul George Jorck and Emma Jorck Foundation.

A CIP catalogue record for this book is available from the British Library

ISBN 978 1 9999928 7 3

Lolli Editions
111 Charterhouse Street
London EC1M 6AW
United Kingdom
www.lollieditions.com

FSC
www.fsc.org
MIX
Paper from
responsible sources
FSC® C103625